Friends
Help Each Other

adapted by Farrah McDoogle

based on the screenplay "Friends Help Each Other" written by Wendy Harris

poses and layouts by Jason Fruchter

Ready-to-Read

Simon Spotlight

New York   London   Toronto   Sydney   New Delhi

SIMON SPOTLIGHT
An imprint of Simon & Schuster Children's Publishing Division
1230 Avenue of the Americas, New York, New York 10020
This Simon Spotlight edition September 2020
© 2014 by The Fred Rogers Company All rights reserved.
All rights reserved, including the right of reproduction in whole or in part in any form.
SIMON SPOTLIGHT, READY-TO-READ, and colophon are registered trademarks of Simon & Schuster, Inc.
For information about special discounts for bulk purchases, please contact
Simon & Schuster Special Sales at 1-866-506-1949 or business@simonandschuster.com.
Manufactured in the United States of America 0522 LAK
10
ISBN 978-1-4814-0368-9 (eBook)
ISBN 978-1-5344-7335-5 (prop)

Hi, neighbor!
Today I am playing
with Katerina Kittycat.

"Meow, Meow!
Do you want to have a
tea party?"
asks Katerina.

"Let me get a chair for you!" says Katerina.

"No, thank you," says Katerina.
"I can do it all by myself."

Oh no!

Katerina bumps the table with the chair.

Everything falls on the floor!

"Maybe Daniel can help!" says Henrietta.

Friends help each other, yes they do.

"Teatime!"
says Katerina.

"I want to pour the tea by myself!"

Oh no!

Katerina spills the tea.

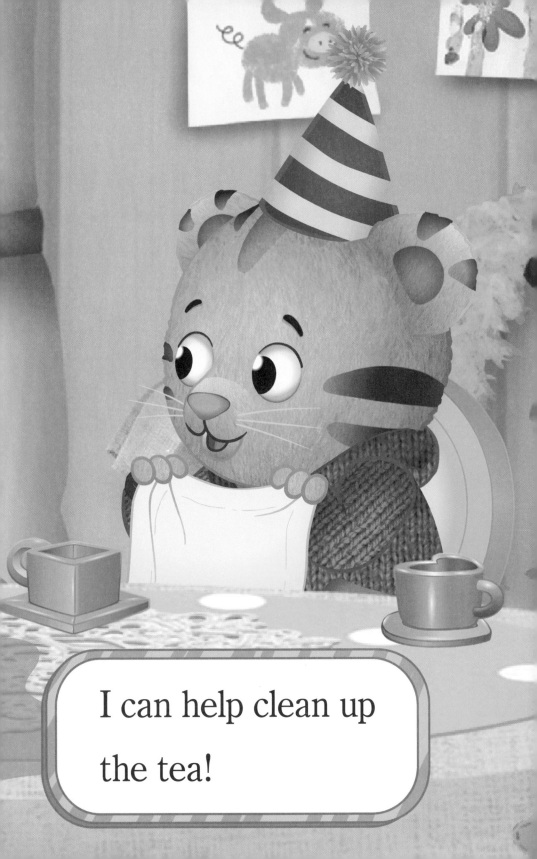

I can help clean up
the tea!

Friends help each other, yes they do!

"Do you want to pour more tea?" asks Henrietta.

"Yes! But this time
I will not do it
all by myself!" says Katerina.

I am happy I helped
my friend today!
Ugga Mugga!